Dear

Wishing you a very fun Christmas, waiting for Santa to come.

Love auntie Claire & uncle Ricky

When you come to Nova Scotia, you can collect sea glass at our beach house!

Sea Glass Summer

Heidi Jardine Stoddart

NIMBUS
PUBLISHING
nimbus.ca

Copyright © 2016, Heidi Jardine Stoddart

All rights reserved. No part of this book may be reproduced, stored in a retrieval system or transmitted in any form or by any means without the prior written permission from the publisher, or, in the case of photocopying or other reprographic copying, permission from Access Copyright, 1 Yonge Street,
Suite 1900, Toronto, Ontario M5E 1E5.

Nimbus Publishing Limited
3731 Mackintosh St, Halifax, NS B3K 5A5
(902) 455-4286 nimbus.ca

Printed and bound in China

NB1186
Design: Heather Bryan

Library and Archives Canada Cataloguing in Publication

Stoddart, Heidi Jardine, 1967-, author, illustrator
Sea glass summer / Heidi Jardine Stoddart.

ISBN 978-1-77108-299-0 (bound)

I. Title.

PS8637.T64S43 2015   jC813'.6   C2014-907765-3

Nimbus Publishing acknowledges the financial support for its publishing activities from the Government of Canada through the Canada Book Fund (CBF) and the Canada Council for the Arts, and from the Province of Nova Scotia. We are pleased to work in partnership with the Province of Nova Scotia to develop and promote our creative industries for the benefit of all Nova Scotians.

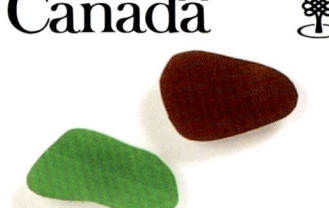

For Gladys, who's always been like a Gram to me.

And with thanks, as ever, to Dwayne.

Molly loved the seashore.

Her favourite place was Gram's cottage by the sea.

Early each morning, after breakfast and tea, Molly and her Gram wandered the beach, looking for sea glass.

The sea glass hid among pebbles, under driftwood, and in the sand. Molly loved blue, and Gram liked green. Gram said Molly was the best finder she'd ever seen.

After lunch, seeking quiet and shade, they'd settle on the porch. Gram knit and watched boats come and go from the harbour. Molly sorted her sea glass, savouring the smooth feel and the soft, colourful glow.

"Some say that sea glass is mermaids' tears," Gram said as she rocked in her chair. "When boats have trouble at sea, the mermaids cry. Those coloured bits are their tears, washed ashore."

Molly looked up, hoping for more mermaid stories, but Gram had already started her nap. Molly added the tiny treasures to her old glass jar.

Often, in the afternoon, Molly and Gram would head back to the beach. Gram liked to have a good float in the ocean every day. She said salt water cured everything. Molly liked splashing, and jumping, and being chased by the waves.

One afternoon, Molly found an unusual rock.

"That's a wishing rock," Gram said. "It has a stripe that goes all the way 'round. Stand with your back to the ocean and toss the rock over your shoulder. Listen for the splash. If the rock makes it back to the sea, your wish will come true."

Molly didn't know what to wish for, so she tucked the rock in her pocket.

At night, Gram tucked Molly into bed with a story and a kiss. Gram propped the window open so Molly could hear the waves, and she set the old jar of sea glass gently on the bedside table, where Molly could see it.

Molly dreamed of ships and sails and mermaid tales.

This was how Molly and Gram liked to spend time together.

That is, until the day the moving truck arrived.

Molly knew it was coming. Her parents had packed up all their things and told her about their new home, far, far away.

When it was time to go, Gram held Molly close.

Molly slipped her wishing rock into Gram's hand.

"What's this?" Gram asked.

"It's a present—a wish waiting to happen."

Gram kept the rock near her heart as they waved goodbye.

Far, far away, Molly unpacked her treasures.

She tried to sleep, but she missed the sound of the waves. Her sea glass glowed in the lights of the city, and Molly thought of Gram.

Soon it was time for school bells and schedules, backpacks and buses.

Geese crossed the sky, heading south, and trees turned autumn orange.

Molly jumble-tumbled in the leaves. Pumpkin patch and jack-o'-lantern glow, Jack Frost sketched on her cold window. Summer faded, and Molly missed Gram.

When dark came early and lingered on, out came Gram's quilt to keep Molly warm.

Winter brought snow and the north wind would blow.

Skating in the park, Molly could see her breath. It looked like fog, and she thought of the sea.

On a still, blue night, the moon icy white, Molly stayed up late, sorting her sea glass. She wondered if the moon was shining over Gram's cottage by the sea.

Then, one blustery afternoon, Molly came home to find a parcel. Gram had knit warm, woolly mitts, just for her. When Molly tried them on, she found a treasure tucked inside. It was her wishing rock, wrapped in a note.

Dear Molly,

A wish waiting to happen!

Love Gram
XOXO

But Molly still didn't know what to wish for. She set the rock on her window ledge.

At last, a muddy smell as rivers swelled, and Canada geese returned.

Icicles were dripping, ropes twirled for skipping, and bicycles appeared.

Fresh breezes blew, and the world seemed new.

Bud green, sprout green, leaf-burst green…Molly thought spring was as green as sea glass, and she wished she were at the beach with Gram. Suddenly, she had an idea.

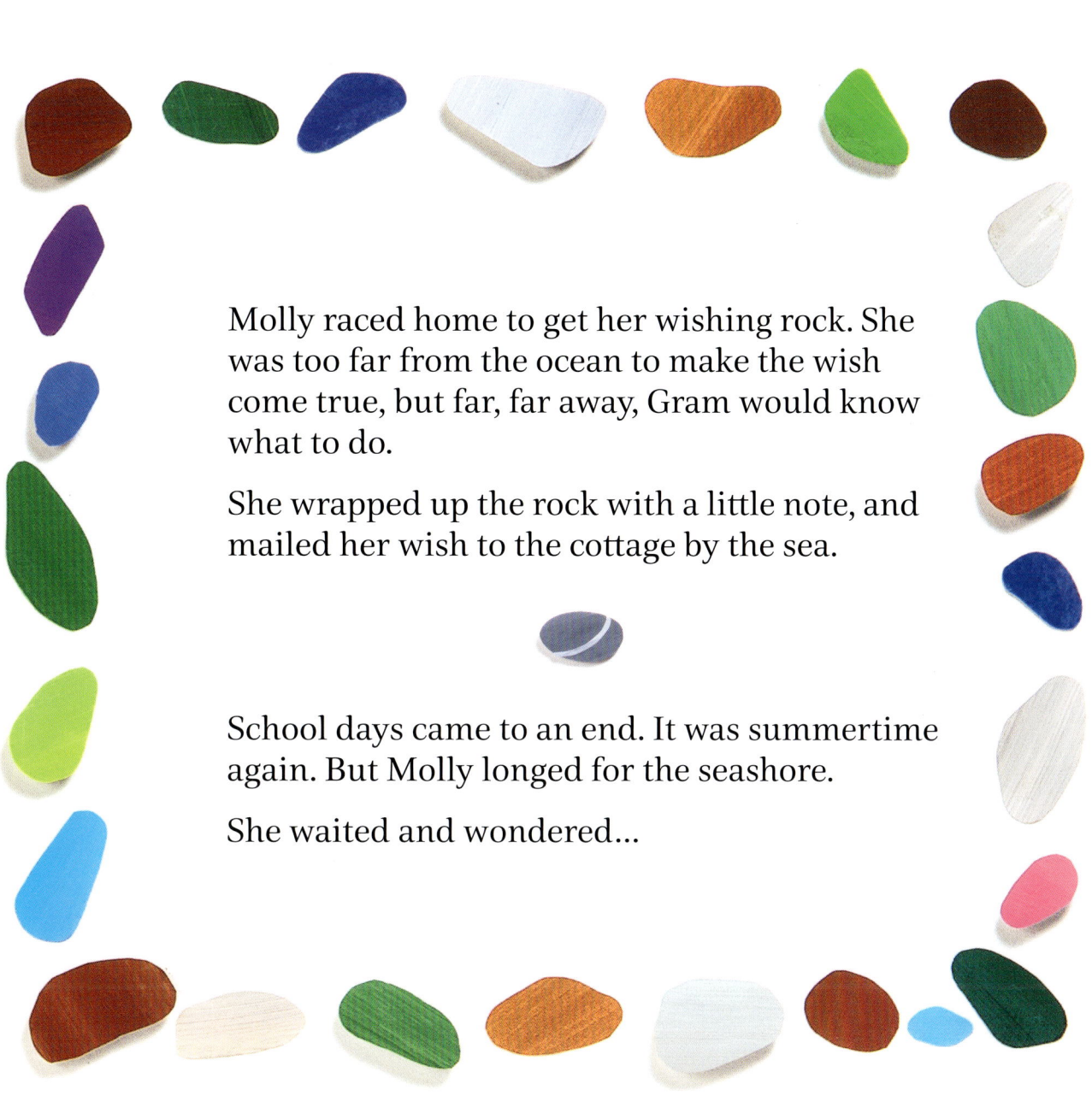

Molly raced home to get her wishing rock. She was too far from the ocean to make the wish come true, but far, far away, Gram would know what to do.

She wrapped up the rock with a little note, and mailed her wish to the cottage by the sea.

School days came to an end. It was summertime again. But Molly longed for the seashore.

She waited and wondered...

...Until one summer day, when Molly found an empty suitcase waiting on her bed. Beside it was a note from Gram: "Our wishing-rock wish has come true!"

Molly packed for her holiday and counted the sleeps.

At last, hugging her old jar of sea glass to keep it safe, she travelled far, far away...

...To her favourite place, where her heart felt at home.
Gram was waiting for her there, in the cottage by the sea.